This 1989 edition published by Derrydale Books,
distributed by Crown Publishers, Inc.,
225 Park Avenue South
New York, N.Y. 10003

Directed by HELENA Productions Ltd.
Illustrated by Van Gool-Lefevre-Loiseaux

Produced by Twin Books
15 Sherwood Place
Greenwich, CT 06830

Printed in Spain by
Printer Industria gráfica sa. Barcelona
D. L. B.: 26785-1989

ISBN 0-517-69318-6

hgfedcba

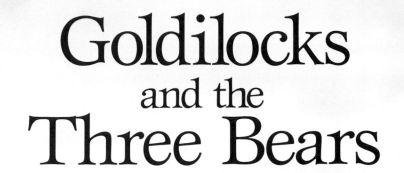

Goldilocks
and the
Three Bears

DERRYDALE BOOKS
New York

Twin Books

On a summer day not so very long ago, a little girl played with her three teddy bears in the shade of a big tree. The girl, who was called Goldilocks, on account of her shiny golden hair, had spent the whole morning in the woods. She and her teddy bear friends had discovered a turtle, several toads, a ladybug, and many patches of pretty flowers. Then they began to feel sleepy and sat down to rest.

"You know," said Goldilocks with a yawn, "I really like those toads we met, and the turtle was awfully cute, but I want to meet some big animals. Maybe a bobcat, or a deer, or some real bears would be nice…" But Goldilocks didn't finish her sentence, because the warm breeze and chirping birds had lulled her to sleep.

Suddenly, Goldilocks heard her mother calling. And because she was a rather naughty girl, and she didn't want to go home, she jumped to her feet and ran deeper into the woods. She clutched her teddy bears as she ran, and though they were cross at being bumped around so, and worried about getting lost, they kept silent.

Before long Goldilocks came to a delightful little house that she had never seen before. Flowers bloomed in window boxes, and there were three doors of different sizes. "I wonder who lives here!" exclaimed Goldilocks.

Goldilocks knocked on the littlest door, but there was no answer. Then she opened the door and went inside. "How adorable!" said Goldilocks.

The house was neat as a pin, and a delicious smell was in the air. Then Goldilocks saw a wooden table with three bowls of porridge on it. Suddenly, she felt quite hungry. She dipped a spoon into the largest bowl, but found the porridge much too hot. Then she tried the middle-sized bowl, but it was too cold.

14

"This is just right!" she exclaimed, sampling porridge from the littlest bowl. And she ate it all up. Her teddy bears sat on the table. They also felt hungry, but were much too polite to eat someone else's food without permission.

"What shall we do next?" asked Goldilocks, gathering up her teddy bears. She peered into the living room and saw three chairs of different sizes. She tossed her teddy bears into the largest chair, and climbed up beside them. "This chair is much too big," she said, dangling her feet over the edge.

Then Goldilocks noticed a middle-sized chair. "Let's try that one," she said to her teddy bears, and they all got into it. "It's not quite right either," she said. Then Goldilocks saw a little chair by the table, and when she sat in it, she found it was just the right size.

She leaned back in the chair and put her feet up on the table, even though she knew it was a naughty thing to do. Suddenly, the chair legs screeched out from under her, and Goldilocks fell over backward. She was not hurt, but the chair broke into several pieces.

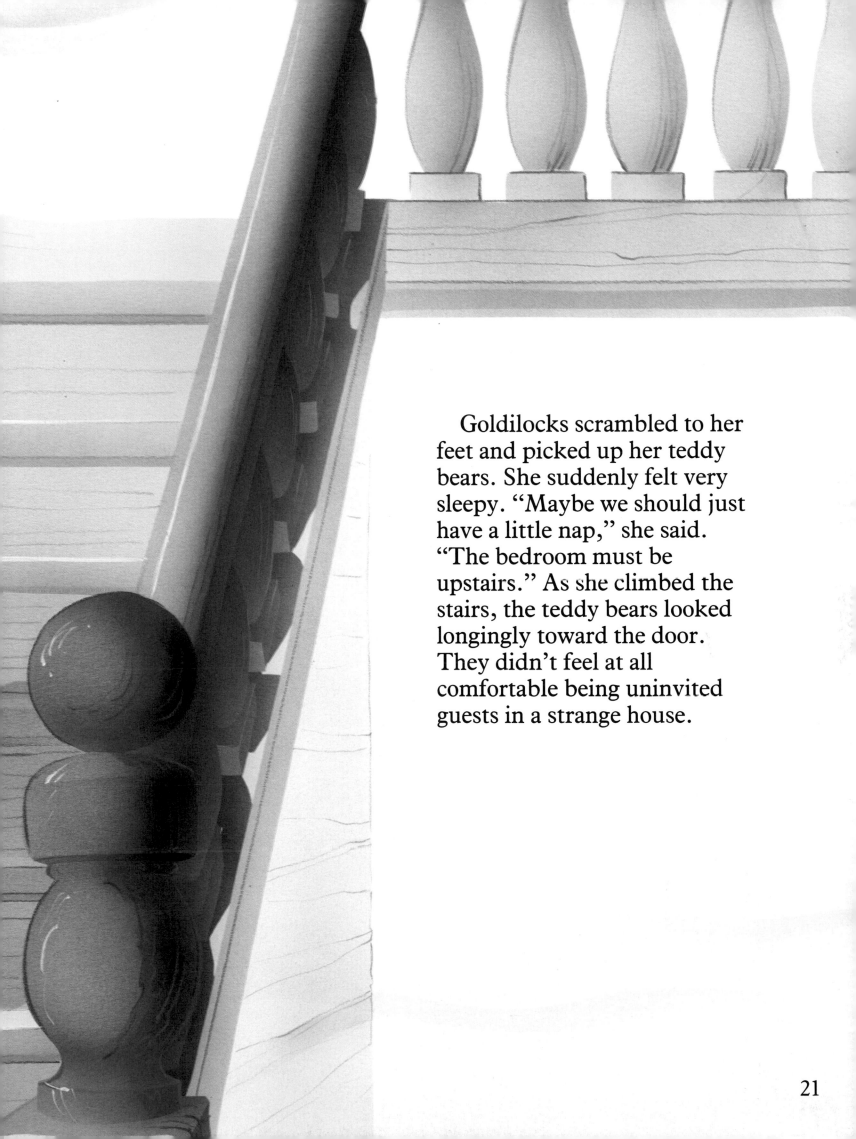

Goldilocks scrambled to her feet and picked up her teddy bears. She suddenly felt very sleepy. "Maybe we should just have a little nap," she said. "The bedroom must be upstairs." As she climbed the stairs, the teddy bears looked longingly toward the door. They didn't feel at all comfortable being uninvited guests in a strange house.

With a little push from Goldilocks' elbow, the bedroom door swung open. There before her were three beds of different sizes. "Look at that!" exclaimed the girl. "Perfect for an afternoon nap."

She ambled down the row of beds. "Let's play house!" she said to her teddy bears. "I'll be the mommy, and you'll be my three little children. You've just brushed your teeth, and now you're ready for bed."

With that, Goldilocks tucked the teddy bears into the smallest bed. "Now I'll sing you a lullabye," she said. She sang so sweetly, and the bed was so comfortable, that the teddy bears soon forgot their worries. They would have drifted off to sleep, but suddenly Goldilocks had another idea.

"Let's have a slumber party!" she exclaimed, pulling the teddy bears out of bed. "We'll tell secrets and have pillow fights and eat popcorn...if we had some."

Goldilocks scrambled onto the largest bed, but it seemed much too hard, even for telling stories. Then she tried the middle-sized bed, but it felt too soft and lumpy. So she flopped onto the smallest bed, and began telling the teddy bears made-up secrets.

In the meantime, the three bears who lived in the house were returning from their midmorning walk. "The porridge must be cool by now," shouted Baby Bear, "and I'm hungry!" He ran ahead as Papa Bear tried to hurry up Mama Bear, who was gathering wildflowers along the way.

But when the bear family approached their house, they knew something was wrong. Mama Bear remembered having closed the door carefully when they went out, yet now the door was ajar. "I'm going to get to the bottom of this," said Papa Bear gruffly. The three bears went quietly inside.

"Oh no!" cried Baby Bear.

"Someone's made a mess of our table," said Papa Bear sternly. "And they've tasted my porridge," he added, glancing into his bowl.

"Someone's been eating my porridge, too," said Mama Bear.

"Someone's been eating my porridge," exclaimed Baby Bear, "and it's all gone!" Sadly, he held his bowl upside down.

34

"Look!" said Papa Bear. "Someone's been sitting in my chair!"
And Mama Bear said, "Someone's been sitting in *my* chair!"
And Baby Bear wailed, "Somebody's been sitting in my chair, and it's all broken to pieces!"

Then Baby Bear had an idea. He rushed to the stairs. "Maybe they're upstairs!" he cried. "Let's catch them!"

"Be careful, son," cautioned Papa Bear. "Wait for us."

The three bears climbed the creaky stairs and opened the bedroom door. "Someone's been sleeping in my bed!" growled Papa Bear.

Mama Bear frowned. "Someone's been sleeping in my bed, too," she said.

Then Baby Bear squealed, "Someone's been sleeping in my bed, and they're all still here!"

The bears' anger at their messy intruder vanished when they saw the sleeping Goldilocks, who looked very innocent. She was curled in Baby Bear's bed with her teddy bears, who were doing their best not to act alarmed. Baby Bear tugged on his mother's skirt and pointed to the girl. "Can we keep her?" he asked. But when Mama Bear scowled back at him, he didn't ask again.

Goldilocks awoke with a start, frightened to see the bears gathered at her bedside. She jumped off the bed and rushed out the door, down the stairs, and out of the house.

She was in such a hurry that she even forgot her teddy bears. Mama Bear, Papa Bear, and Baby Bear rushed after her, shouting things like, "Wait! We won't harm you!" and "Come back and make us fresh porridge!" But Goldilocks' only thought was to get away.

"What a close call!" she thought, as she ran through the woods, "Mother would be so angry with me if she knew..." And suddenly she could hear her mother calling.

Goldilocks sat up and stretched. "Coming, Mother!" she called.
Then she looked at her teddy bears. "What a strange dream I had,"
she said. "But that's all right. You're here!" And the teddy bears
wondered what they had done to deserve the big hug she gave them.